Winnie's
Problem Pets

LAURA OWEN & KORKY PAUL

OXFORD
UNIVERSITY PRESS

Helping your child to read

Before they start

★ Talk about the back cover blurb. What kinds of problems do you think Wilbur and Scruff will give Winnie in these stories?

★ Look at the cover picture. Does it give any clues about what might happen in these stories?

During reading

★ Let your child read at their own pace, either silently or out loud.

★ If necessary, help them work out words they don't know by saying each sound out loud and then blending them together to say the word, e.g. *b-a-n-d-a-ge-s, bandages.*

★ Encourage your child to keep checking that the text makes sense and they understand what they are reading. Remind them to reread to check the meaning if they're not sure.

★ Give them lots of praise for good reading!

After reading

★ Look at page 48 for some fun activities.

Contents

OXFORD
UNIVERSITY PRESS

Great Clarendon Street, Oxford OX2 6DP
Oxford University Press is a department of the University of Oxford.
It furthers the University's objective of excellence in research, scholarship,
and education by publishing worldwide. Oxford is a registered trade mark
of Oxford University Press in the UK and in certain other countries

"Itchy Witchy" was first published in *Winnie Says Cheese* 2009
"Winnie's Perfect Pet" was first published in *Winnie the Twit* 2009
This edition published 2018

British Library Cataloguing in Publication Data

Data available

ISBN: 978-0-19-276526-0

3 5 7 9 10 8 6 4

OX27868901

Printed in China

Paper used in the production of this book is a natural,
recyclable product made from wood grown in sustainable forests.
The manufacturing process conforms to the environmental
regulations of the country of origin.

Acknowledgements
With thanks to Catherine Baker for editorial support

Itchy
Witchy

✦ Chapter ✦ One

Winnie's mobile phone rang. **Brrring!**
Brrring! Winnie picked it up, and groaned.
Her sister was calling.

"I'm taking Wayne to the witches' cat
show tomorrow, Winnie," she shrieked. "He
won it last year, you know."

"Have you still got that scraggy old cat
thing of yours, Winnie?" she asked.

"He's called Wilbur," said Winnie. "And
he's lovely."

"Well, we'll see how lovely he is at
the show, won't we! Hee hee!" laughed
Winnie's sister.

"No," said Winnie. "I wasn't going to—"

"Hee hee!" her sister cackled. "I knew it!
I knew you wouldn't dare put Wilbur in for
the show, because you know very well he'll
come last! Hee hee! I just knew it!"

Winnie stared crossly at the phone.
"Well, you knew wrong!" she said. "Wilbur
will be in the show, and he might just win it!
So there!"

Winnie put the phone down. Then
she started feeling worried. "Oh, banana
bandages!" she said to herself. "What have
I gone and done now?"

Winnie looked at Wilbur lying happily in the sun. There was a spider's web stuck between Wilbur's ears. There was a bald patch on his back where he'd lost some of his fur. There was some pond slime hanging from his tail. And flies were hovering all around him, because he smelled.

Winnie found a pair of scissors, some carpet shampoo, a big bottle of skunk scent, a brush, a comb, and some slug-slime hair gel. She took them all outside.

"Oh, Wilbur!" she called.

Wilbur opened one eye.

"Come to Winnie, Wilbur!" called Winnie in a sing-song voice.

Wilbur leaped up, and he was about to run when ...

"**Abracadabra!**" went Winnie, and instantly poor Wilbur was frozen still. "I'm sorry about this, Wilbur, but I've got to make you beautiful," said Winnie.

Winnie got to work, washing and combing. But then she saw a little something **hop-hop-HOP** in Wilbur's fur.

Chapter Two

"Oh, toads' toenails, Wilbur, you've got
fleas!" said Winnie. She caught a flea
mid-hop and popped it into her mouth.
"Mmm," she said. "It's quite tasty in a tickle
your tastebuds kind of way, but you won't
win the show if you've got fleas. Come on,
Wilbur. We're off to the vet's to get you
some flea medicine."

Winnie unfroze Wilbur and put him in the carrying box. It was horrible being in the box. Wilbur felt the jolting and swaying as Winnie got off her broomstick and carried the box into the surgery.

As soon as he smelled the surgery and the vet, he started howling.

"Meeeeooooowww!" howled Wilbur, miserably.

"My goodness," said the vet. "When did this animal last get a check-up?"

"Oh, ages ago," said Winnie. "He hates coming here."

"Meeow!" agreed Wilbur, and then, to prove it, he climbed up the vet and sat on his head. When Winnie lifted him down, he sank his claws into the vet's wig.

"What was that bird's nest doing on your head?" Winnie asked the vet.

The vet squirted stuff onto Wilbur to
get rid of the fleas. The fleas coughed
and sneezed. They all marched off Wilbur
and straight onto Winnie and the vet. *Itch-
itch, scratch.*

"Now," said the vet. *Itch, scratch.* "This
cat needs injections for cat flu and cat cold
and cat sore throat and cat tennis elbow."

"Are you sure?" said Winnie. "How much will that lot cost?"

"Let me see," said the vet, and he began tapping numbers on his calculator. **Itch, scratch**. Winnie saw the numbers getting bigger and bigger.

"Quick, Wilbur!" she whispered. "Let's go!"

✦ Chapter ✦ Three

When they got to the show, Wilbur looked very smart, but not very happy. Winnie felt worried and itchy-witchy scratchy.

But Winnie's sister and her cat were as smug as a bug. Wayne lounged about, smiling like a film star.

"What do you think of my Wayne, then, Winnie? Just feel how silky his fur is!" said Winnie's sister.

So Winnie felt Wayne's fur. And as she touched him, all the fleas hopped off Winnie and onto Wayne. **Itch-itch, scratch. Itch-itch-itch, scritchety-scratch.**

"Ooh, here comes the judge! Just watch what he says about Wayne and Wilbur, hee hee!" said her sister.

Itch-scratch, went Wayne.

"Don't do that, Wayne darling," said Winnie's sister. "Be nice for the judge."

The judge poked at Wilbur first.

"Meeow!" went Wilbur. He'd had enough of being poked for one day.

The judge lifted Wilbur's tail.

"Hiss!" **Scratch!** went Wilbur.

"Ouch!" yelled the judge. "What a terrible cat!"

"Hee hee!" said Winnie's sister.

Then the judge poked at Wayne.

"Purr!" went Wayne.

The judge lifted Wayne's tail.

"Purr!" went Wayne, again.

"Very nice indeed," said the judge. "What a fine and healthy cat this seems to be."

But just then, Wayne felt itchy. *Itch-itch, scratch-scratch*. And then the judge felt an itch and began to scratch, too.

"Urgh!" he shouted, jumping away from Wayne. "This cat has FLEAS!"

He was about to send Wayne away, but there was no need to because everybody else was running and shoving to get away from the leaping fleas and the show.

Soon there were no witches or cats left at the show.

"What a lot of fuss over a few fleas!" said Winnie, happily scratching herself. "Call themselves witches? Huh! Come on, let's go home, Wilbur."

Back home Wilbur rolled in the grass to get himself nice and dirty again.

"Here's a rosette for you!" said Winnie. "You're *my* best cat!"

"Purr!" said Wilbur proudly.

All the fleas that had hopped onto
Winnie's head went back onto Wilbur,
because Wilbur tasted nicer, if you were
a flea.

Soon, all Wilbur's fleas were back.
Except for one adventurous flea who had
hopped onto Winnie's sister because he liked
the taste of her hairspray. So she was still
going **itch-itch, scritchety-scratch.**

Hee hee!

Winnie's Perfect Pet

⋆ Chapter ⋆
One

Wilbur was asleep on the front doorstep when Winnie rushed up.

"Oh, Wilbur!" she said. "I've had a terrible morning! Mrs Parmar asked me to help the children learn their spellings, but I thought she said spells! I showed them how to magic up a dragon. It was only a little one, but now Mrs P is cross with me. The dragon set off all the fire alarms!"

Wilbur opened one eye. He looked at Winnie, then he closed the eye again.

"Let's play a game, Wilbur," said Winnie. "Take my mind off things. That's what a good pet would do."

Wilbur arched his back and yawned.

"You're as lazy as a lizard!" said Winnie. "Come on, let's play tennis, Wilbur!"

Winnie rushed indoors. She opened the cupboard under the stairs, and out fell … everything!

First Winnie tugged at something grey
and tatty. Then she pulled out something
that looked like a spoon tied up with string,
and something else that looked like a
mouldy old apple.

She popped off to change … and then skipped back outside.

"What do you think of my outfit, Wilbur?" she asked.

Wilbur just put his paws over his face.

Winnie bounced the ball all around Wilbur. **Bounce, bounce.** "Come on," she said. "You're no fun, Wilbur. I'll have to use magic, if you won't play."

Winnie pointed her wand at the racquet and ball. "**Abracadabra, abracadabra, abracadabra!**" she shouted.

In an instant, there were three tennis racquets. The racquets were hitting balls at Winnie.

Winnie waved her own racquet all over the place, but she missed every ball.

"Ow! Get off! Stop!" she shouted. "Newts' kneecaps! Nobody's nice to me today, not even my wand!"

Winnie threw her wand as far as she could. A moment later, the wand was back … in the mouth of a dog.

✦ Chapter ✦ Two

The dog came bounding up to Winnie.
It was Scruff, who belonged to Jerry the
giant who lived next door to Winnie. Scruff
dropped the wand at Winnie's feet. Then he
grinned up at her and wagged his tail.

"Good boy, Scruff," said Winnie. "Do you
want me to throw it again?"

Winnie threw the wand again, and again, and again. And each time, Scruff dashed back with it. Winnie threw the ball, too.

"Fetch, Scruff!" she said. "Clever boy! Did you see that, Wilbur? Isn't he a clever dog?"

"Meeow," said Wilbur. He didn't sound very impressed.

Soon it was lunchtime, and they all went into the kitchen. Wilbur winked at Scruff and pointed at a packet of kipper biscuits. He nodded towards Winnie. Scruff grinned and nodded his head and wagged his tail. He took the biscuit box in his mouth and gave it to Winnie.

"For me?" said Winnie, not really looking. "Thank you, Scruff!"

Winnie took a biscuit from the box and popped it into her mouth.

"Ew! Pah!" Winnie spat the biscuit out. "Yuck! I hate kipper biscuits!"

Scruff hid under the table.

Wilbur grinned. Then he put all Winnie's favourite lunch snacks on a tray. Crispy worms. A nettle sandwich. A cup of slug smoothie.

"Yummy!" said Winnie. "You're cleverer than Scruff, Wilbur. You know just what I like!"

But Scruff stuck out a leg and … **Trip!** went Wilbur.

Crash! went the tray.

Splat! went the smoothie, and crispy worms fell all over Winnie.

"Oh, Wilbur, you're as clumsy as a centipede on skates!" shouted Winnie.

Wilbur and Scruff stuck their tongues out at each other.

Suddenly, Winnie had a brilliant idea.

"Of course!" said Winnie. "Cats are clever and dogs are obedient. I want a pet that's both of those things, so what I need is a cog!"

"Yowl!" went Scruff.

"Meeow!" went Wilbur.

They both raced for the door. They both wanted to be the first one to escape outside.

But before they got there, Winnie said, "Abracadabra!"

★ Chapter ★ Three

Magic whirled and swirled, and suddenly there was … a cog.

"Perfect," said Winnie.

But the cog was not perfect. It ran up the curtains and chewed them to bits.

"MEEOW-WOOF!"

Chew-chew, munch. Chew. Munch.

The cog jumped down and stood at Winnie's feet.

"Be a good cog," said Winnie. But the cog
hissed at her. Then it did a wee on her foot.

"Yuck! Bad cog!" said Winnie.

The cog jumped out of the window into
the garden. It began to dig.

"Stop!" shouted Winnie.

The cog took no notice. It rolled in the mud. Then it sat and licked the mud off its legs. It jumped up at Winnie with muddy paws and scratchy claws.

"Get down!" said Winnie. "Naughty boy! Wilbur, save me!"

But of course, Wilbur wasn't there.

"Oh dear," said Winnie. "I wanted to mix the best bits of a cat with the best bits of a dog. This cog is the worst bits of both! Where's my wand? I want my Wilbur back."

Winnie saw her wand on the ground. The cog saw it too, and it began to run towards it, teeth snip-snapping.

"It's my wand!" shouted Winnie, and she leaped to grab it. "**Abracadabra!**" She waved the wand just as the cog's teeth were about to snap it in two.

Suddenly, Wilbur was back, looking shocked but pleased. And Scruff was back, too. He ran away down the drive.

"Scruff!" boomed a big voice. It was Jerry the giant.

Scruff jumped around his owner, wagging his tail and woofing.

"My dear old Scruff!" laughed Jerry. "I wondered where you'd got to! You're the best dog in the world!"

Winnie smiled and picked Wilbur up. "Well, if Scruff's the best dog, you're definitely the best cat. Better than that cog, any day! Give us a kiss, Wilbur!"

After reading activities

Quick quiz

See how fast you can answer these questions! Look back at the stories if you can't remember.

1. In "Itchy Witchy", where do Wilbur's fleas go when the vet gets rid of them?

2. In "Winnie's Perfect Pet", where does Scruff live?

3. In "Winnie's Perfect Pet", what does Winnie think of the kipper biscuits Scruff gives her?

1. onto Winnie and the vet. 2. with Winnie's next-door neighbour, Jerry the giant. 3. she thinks they're disgusting.

Talk about it!

★ If you could have any animal in the world as a pet, what would you choose? Draw a picture of your perfect pet, give it a name and write a few sentences to describe it.